Kingsley Trunk

Books by L. Sydney Abel

Gruvel the Great
Ish-ish Ishbochernay
Keypya and the Pirates
Kingsley Trunk
Marge and the Wobbly Onkey
Mr. Runkin's Secret
Patrick Duck
Smelly Nelly Welly
The Evergreen Wolf

Kingsley Trunk

L. Sydney Abel

SPEAKING VOLUMES, LLC
NAPLES, FLORIDA
2018

Kingslely Trunk

ISBN 978-1-62815-517-4

For the whisperer in my ear

With thanks to the angel sent—my soul saver

Thank you Karen for your patience and understanding

Table of Contents

Spider 🕷 One

Victor should have been asleep like all other eight-year-olds. But he wasn't. He was sat up in bed, reading a comic by moonbeam light.

Downstairs, the hall clock struck twelve. The witching hour, as if by magic, made the moon brighter.

Victor's half-drawn curtains let even brighter moonlight in. Moonbeams shone over his bed and across his floor and up his wall.

Suddenly, something black crept across his floor...

It cast a frightening shadow...

Afraid, Victor rolled up his comic and whacked the floor with such a WHACK that it made a tiny spider stop stone-dead. The tiny spider's teensy-weensy heart almost stopped.

Victor again brought his comic crashing down, this time ready to land right on top of the tiny spider.

Without warning, a flash of light appeared and the spider was gone.

"You're safe now, tiny spider," said a voice that seemed to come from nowhere. "Don't be afraid. Everything will be alright."

Victor felt a dragonfly brush his cheek as he stood within twinkling silver and blue lights, and wondered where the spider had gone.

Early that morning, when it was still dark outside, Kingsley Trunk came down his stairs wearing a blue dressing gown and square-shaped slippers.

Kingsley Trunk was an elephant and was special in many ways. He was four magical feet and seven magical inches tall, and was about to make a hot drink.

Kingsley was always very precise. His routine started by firstly filling the kettle with fresh cold water-that was an outright must. Secondly, it was the lighting of the gas ring.

A blue dancing flame always made him smile as he put the kettle on to boil. It was now that he put a heaped spoonful of tea, which his great-uncle had sent all the way from India, into his yellow teapot. Thirdly, after the kettle blew its whistle, boiling hot water was poured into the teapot. The tea leaves seemed to sing to Kingsley in their two minute brew. Lastly, he poured himself the perfect mug of tea. He never added milk or sugar; he thought tea should taste only of tea.

In the safe hands of a Spider Fairy, a tiny spider shook with fear.

This Fairy was the colour of a raincloud. She was very beautiful and so faint to our eyes that you could hardly see her.

Through the air, above cities and towns and villages, she flew–gently cradling the tiny spider from harm. When, finally, into her view came a very special place. There, all alone, almost hidden by trees, was the house of Kingsley Trunk.

Not everyone could see this house of red bricks, with its vegetable garden to the back and rose garden to the front. Only those that needed to could.

The dawn was coming, and the birds were waking up to chirp in a new day.

Kingsley stood by his back door–listening–as he did every day of the year. As the birds started to sing, all around began to get lighter as a lemon-coloured sun climbed the morning sky.

The Spider Fairy landed as softly as a dragonfly. From somewhere between the runner beans and the lettuce patch, she called out, "Kingsley!"

Carefully, and ever so slightly, she opened her fingers and peered in at what she'd been carrying. The tiny spider was tightly curled up, resembling a little black pea. It was then, with a gentle skip, that the Spider Fairy made her way towards her special elephant.

Kingsley excitedly jumped up and down, and blew a trumpeting sound through his waving trunk.

"Have you brought another one?" he said, giving a beaming smile. He was so overjoyed that he almost forgot his manners. Then he remembered, and bowed very politely to Miranda the Spider Fairy.

Kingsley Trunk

Spider ❧ Two

Miranda followed Kingsley into the kitchen; it was only big enough for a cupboard, a table and two chairs, an enchanted elephant and an enchanting Spider Fairy, and of course, the occasional visitor.

"Please sit down," said Kingsley, putting his empty mug into the sink.

Kingsley loved his sink. It was the perfect place for washing his vegetables. Also, it was positioned under the window that overlooked the garden. The windowsill was a place where pupils slept.

Kingsley took a goblet—which was made by the frozen folk who live under the Ice Mountains near the top of the world—from the cupboard; he poured into it some of his prized gooseberry juice. Whatever was poured into the goblet became very cold, and remained very cold, forever. Spider Fairies, for some magical reason, only drank ice-cold drinks.

Miranda sat on her usual chair, which was piled high with gardening books. She was now almost the same height as Kingsley.

"I have another one for you," she said, as she unfurled her hands to reveal the tiny spider within. She then blew softly over the tiny spider, giving it the power of speech.

Kingsley's eyes shone.

Miranda gently put the tiny spider on the table, and sipped at her gooseberry juice. "This is truly scrumptious," she said. "It's just what I needed after those long hours of flying."

Kingsley beamed with pride.

The tiny spider trembled by the yellow teapot and wondered if this strange creature had a rolled-up comic somewhere, and if so, was it going to use it?

"This tiny spider is very nervous," said Miranda softly. "A boy called Victor tried to squash it with a rolled-up comic," she explained.

"But it's just a spider," said Kingsley, peering over the teapot.

"Sometimes, boys and girls get frightened. They don't realise that the spider is also frightened," said Miranda, smiling down at the tiny spider. "Then there are those boys and girls that are just plain cruel. Those vile children will one day grow up to be vile adults. We can only hope that vile Victor will change his ways."

Miranda finished her drink–every drop. At that point she vanished in a flash of light that sparked silver and blue.

Kingsley still had trouble understanding that Miranda could

come and go with a flash of light, but had to fly when others were with her. One day he hoped to ask her why.

Gently, Kingsley lifted up the teapot and emptied its contents into a bucket under the sink. He said, as softly as he could, without making any excited trumpeting calls, "My name is Kingsley, I'm an elephant, and I'm here to help you.

Spider Three

In the silence that followed, Kingsley waited patiently for the tiny spider to say something. The tiny spider didn't utter one word.

"Suffering frogs' teeth!" said Kingsley. "This won't do at all."

Still the tiny spider uttered nothing.

"Are you a boy spider or a girl spider?" said Kingsley. "I'm sorry to ask, but you're so small and I haven't heard your voice, so it's difficult to tell."

"I'm a boy spider," stated the tiny spider, trembling nervously.

"Of course you are," said Kingsley. "And now that you can talk I'm going to give you a name."

Kingsley remembered all the names he'd given. He was careful not to pick one that another spider had. Finally, he thought of a name.

"I'm going to call you Burrton," he said, and smiled.

"I like that," said the tiny spider.

"I thought you would," said Kingsley. "Now, Burrton," continued Kingsley, with a gleam in his eye, "is there anything you'd like to ask me?" He knew there must be, because there always was.

"Where am I?" asked Burrton.

"You're in my home," answered Kingsley.

"What happened?" asked Burrton.

"You were going to be made squishy squashy flat," explained Kingsley. "Luckily for you, the Spider Fairy came just in the nick of time."

Burrton trembled. "When can I go home?" he asked.

"Soon," said Kingsley. "But first you have to learn things."

"What sort of things?" asked Burrton.

"I'll tell you later," said Kingsley.

Kingsley went to the cupboard and took out his favourite fruit cake. He cut himself a big chunk and placed some small crumbly pieces in front of Burrton.

Burrton was hungry. He ate and ate till his tummy was fit to burst.

Afterwards, Kingsley went upstairs to get dressed. He hung his blue dressing gown behind the bathroom door, slipped off his square-shaped slippers, and removed his pyjamas. He did his routine of washing in all the right places, including brushing his teeth and tusks. He then put on a tee-shirt and dungarees.

Kingsley made his bed and came downstairs.

Spider  Four

And so the lessons began...

Kingsley fetched drawing paper, a charcoal pencil, and an eraser from the desk drawer in the front room. He placed the paper next to Burrton, so he could see, and sat down at the table.

"Okay, Burrton, now we can begin," he said.

Burrton looked nervous.

Kingsley drew a circle, about the size of a milk bottle top, on the uppermost half of the paper. He then drew eight legs and eight eyes.

"That's you, Burrton," said Kingsley.

"That's not me," stated Burrton.

"Yes, it is," replied Kingsley, who was very pleased with his latest attempt at drawing a spider. He was getting a whole lot better at doing a round squiggle with lines and dots.

"If he's me and I'm me, then who's the real me?" asked Burrton, examining the pancake-flat him.

"You're the real you," answered Kingsley. "Thank goodness this is only a drawing of you. If you'd been hit by that rolled-up comic, you'd be just as flat," said Kingsley, and continuing to draw, added a stick boy.

Burrton trembled.

Kingsley looked at Burrton and smiled. "There are 4 rules of spider survival," he said. "The first rule is: if you see anyone or hear anyone, you must always stay hidden. Rule 1: stay hidden."

Burrton looked up at Kingsley and called out, "Rule 1: stay hidden."

"That's right," said Kingsley. "The second rule is: if you're seen, you should never stay still. Always keep moving and remember to try and get into the shadows as soon as possible. Rule 2: keep moving."

Burrton looked up at Kingsley and called out, "Rule 2: keep moving."

"Right again," said Kingsley, as he drew an arrow pointing which way Burrton should go.

"Shall we continue?" asked Kingsley.

Burrton nodded.

Kingsley looked at Burrton, smiled and said, "The third rule is: if for any reason someone comes near you, you are to run straight at them. Rule 3: run at them."

"WHAT?" cried Burrton.

"They're more frightened than you are," said Kingsley reassuringly. "That's why they try to squash you." He began rubbing out the first arrow with the eraser, before adding another arrow—only this time coming from the spider to the boy. He finished his drawing by giving the boy a rolled-up comic.

"B-B-But to run at them!" said Burrton. "Won't that make them want to squash me even more?"

"You would think so, wouldn't you? But they won't, they'll jump a mile," said Kingsley, who began laughing so loud that his trunk sounded like a bugle. It was a good job his trunk was pointing upwards or he might have blown the tiny spider clean off the table. After he blew his last note, he added, "But you only run at them if you see no other way of escape. I promise it'll work, it always does. Now, would Kingsley lie to you?"

"I hope not," said Burrton, wanting desperately to believe everything this elephant said. "Rule 1: stay hidden. Rule 2: keep moving. Rule 3: run at them."

Burrton gave his legs a wiggle and jumped forward.

Kingsley didn't jump. He wasn't frightened of spiders.

15

"Yes, that's 1, 2, and 3," said Kingsley. "You're doing excellent." He quickly drew a frightened stick boy and a running away spider at the bottom of the paper. This made the tiny spider laugh.

Burrton felt very pleased. He wasn't feeling half as nervous as he had been earlier. He looked at the drawings again and studied them carefully. He also kept going over the rules in his head.

Kingsley waited a while, allowing Burrton to think.

"What's rule number 4?" asked Burrton.

"The fourth rule is really easy," said Kingsley. "Ready?"

"Yes," answered Burrton.

"Okay. Now when they jump or flinch or scream or even run away, that's your chance. You must take this moment to get away and hide," said Kingsley. "Remember to stay hidden. They may come looking for you. Rule 4: hide and stay hidden."

"Are you sure it will work?" asked Burrton.

"Yes, of course it will," said Kingsley. "But it's best not to be seen in the first place, isn't it?"

"Rule 1: never be seen," said Burrton.

"That's right," said Kingsley. "Never be seen." He jumped up and down, and gave a little toot on his trunk, just to show how happy he was.

Spider 🕷 Five

Kingsley tidied away by putting the drawing paper, pencil, and eraser back into the desk drawer. He picked up his drawing, which Burrton was sat on, and very carefully placed it onto the kitchen windowsill.

Burrton could now see the outside world. He saw candyfloss clouds drifting in a pale blue sky. Sunflowers were standing tall; their yellow faces turned towards the sun as if sunbathing, seemingly smiling as they swayed.

Kingsley did the washing up.

Burrton's thoughts went to the other him and the boy holding a rolled-up comic. He shuddered at the thought of how squishy squashy flat he looked and that it could have happened to him if it wasn't for the Spider Fairy.

Kingsley made everything tidy. The pots were put away. The table top was given a wipe over; crumbs were thrown out for the birds.

"You're very organized," said Burrton.

"There's a place for everything," stated Kingsley.

"Including me?" asked Burrton.

"Yes, including you," answered Kingsley, with a reassuring smile.

"Vile Victor didn't think that," said Burrton.

"He was wrong," said Kingsley.

"Vile Victor wouldn't agree," replied Burrton, remembering the rolled-up comic again.

"No, you're probably right," admitted Kingsley. "Hopefully, one day, he'll understand. In the meantime, just remember the rules I've taught you. I'm going into the garden now; I've got one or two things I must do," he said, putting on his square-shaped rubber gardening boots.

Burrton looked again at the drawing. *That vile Victor will never understand how wrong he is,* he thought. *If I were a thousand times bigger, I would flatten him. I bet he wouldn't like that! Oh dear! Then I'll be big bad Burrton!*

At the bottom of Kingsley's garden were rows of gooseberry bushes. They had yellow-green berries that would soon become gooseberry juice.

Kingsley knelt and stirred a bucketful of cold tea, which he'd carried from the kitchen.

"Lovely stuff," he said, as a brown froth formed. Then, very carefully, he poured the mixture around the roots of his gooseberry bushes. He couldn't be sure, but he thought he heard the bushes say thank you.

Kingsley set about his other gardening jobs. He tied up the beans and watered them. Then, he checked his cabbages and emptied the slug traps over the wall. He didn't want to hurt the slugs, for he knew they'd be back in a day or two or even faster-it depended on how hungry they were. He was so used to seeing them that he was thinking about giving them names. The big black glistening one seemed to be the leader-he was always first back over the wall. There was never a nibble out of the deliberately planted dandelions.

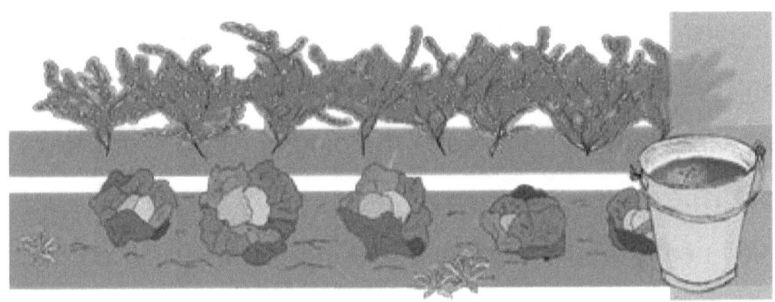

Back on the windowsill, Burrton was still studying the drawing while practising the rules over and over in his head. *Rule 1: never be seen. Rule 2: keep moving. Rule 3: run at them. Rule 4: hide and stay hidden.*

Kingsley worked hard in his garden.

Every half hour he had a short rest. And so it went on—working and resting until all the jobs were done.

Spider Six

Kingsley had worked up an appetite and was ready for his evening meal. He returned to his kitchen and washed his hands.

"Are you hungry, Burrton?" he asked, as he started to peel the potatoes.

"Not really," said Burrton, looking gloomy. "When can I go home?"

"You mustn't worry about that now, tomorrow's another day. Today is learn and remember. We'll see about you going home tomorrow. In the morning, and only if you can remember what I've taught you, I'll contact Miranda," said Kingsley, chopping cabbage.

Burrton felt happier, but only slightly. *What if I forget the rules by then*, he thought, *then the elephant won't contact the fairy. What if I can't remember them, ever? Will I have to stay here forever?*

Kingsley prepared the meal. He put cut potatoes into a pan of cold water, and added a dash of salt. Then he lit the gas; the blue dancing flames again made him smile as he put the pan on to boil. As the water began to bubble volcanically he turned the gas down so the potatoes could simmer.

After ten minutes, Kingsley put another pan of water on to boil. When this pan began to bubble volcanically, he dropped in the chopped cabbage. After five boiling cabbage minutes, the meal was ready.

The pans were drained of water. The potatoes were mashed and dolloped onto a large plate. On top of the mash was piled the cabbage. From a jar labelled 'homemade tomato sauce' Kingsley dribbled swirly, orange lines over his steaming mash and cabbage.

A refreshing drink of cider was poured. Thought was given to Burrton, but the idea of a wobbly spider on the windowsill soon put a stop to it.

"Are you sure you're not hungry?" asked Kingsley.

"I'm feeling a little hungry," admitted Burrton. "Could I have some more cake?"

Kingsley took some fruit cake from the cupboard and put it next to Burrton.

Burrton tucked in. He was developing a liking for fruit cake.

Kingsley thought the whiff of cabbage smelt stupendous. Unfortunately, his spider visitors had the opposite view. To them, cabbage smelt of a smelly loo.

Kingsley sat at the table and shovelled forkful after forkful of steaming mash and cabbage into his mouth. His trunk acted like a chimney, letting out steam.

Soon his plate was empty. Kingsley gave a satisfied smile. He gulped a big mouthful of cider and burped bubbles through his trunk, which fizzed and popped like fire crackers.

Burrton watched in wonder.

Kingsley finished off his meal with some of his favourite fruit cake. Burrton couldn't eat anymore; his tiny body was bursting at the seams.

The evening beckoned the elephant to come into the garden, to watch the end of the day. Kingsley picked up his glass of cider and went outside. As he stood there the sun started to turn the sky red as it slowly descended over the orchard apple trees. A happy elephant drank his cider. There was more fizzing and popping as he thought about tomorrow. *I must do some cleaning, and then I must attend to the front garden. Those roses are looking a bit shabby. I hate deadheading and I hate pruning. Come to think of it, I hate vacuuming and I hate polishing. I know... I'll dig up the roses and plant more cabbages.*

As Kingsley pondered, the sun became so low in the red sky that it cast the house into shade. "Brrr!" he said, "I think it's time I went in."

Kingsley put on the light. He did the washing up and took the potato peelings and cabbage stalks down to his compost heap.

Back over the wall travelled the slugs. A silver trail glistened behind them.

"Hello, Blackie," said Kingsley. He could have sworn he heard the others saying 'Follow him, he knows the way.'

Kingsley returned to the kitchen.

Burrton was studying hard. He was silently mouthing the rules of survival as he looked at the other him running towards his attacker.

"It's time for my favourite goggle-box programme," said Kingsley. "Would you like to watch it with me?"

"Yes," said Burrton.

Burrton was carried into the front room, where the goggle-box stood. It was switched on.

Kingsley sat in his armchair. Burrton sat on a cushion on the settee.

The news was being broadcast; Kingsley didn't always like the news. Too many sad things in the world made him feel unhappy.

When the news finished, the weather forecast came on. A man talked in front of a map with suns everywhere.

"It's another fine day tomorrow," said Kingsley.

The weatherman wished everyone good evening by saying, "Enjoy the sun while you can, because torrential downpours are on the way."

"Suffering frogs' teeth!" said Kingsley. "Too much rain might damage my vegetables. What about the slugs? They might get washed away. Not forgetting the sunflowers, they won't like it one little bit."

Kingsley's complaining wouldn't change anything. What he needed was a giant umbrella. Unfortunately he didn't know any giants.

"What is suffering frogs' teeth?" Burrton asked.

"Frogs with toothache," Kingsley answered. "I shoo those tooth-aching frogs to the bottom of the garden because they are screeching in terrible agony. I say suffering frogs' teeth when I'm unhappy about something, just like the frogs are unhappy."

"The frogs are unhappy because they are frightened, that's why they screech," said Burrton. "Frogs don't get toothache, silly."

"Well I never," stated Kingsley. "You learn something new every day."

"What do you say when there's something you're happy about?" asked Burrton.

"I say jumping elephants, because elephants jump up and down when they're happy," answered Kingsley.

The long-awaited broadcast started...

"Have you ever wondered what's out there?" said the voice from the goggle-box. "Tonight, you are going to see unidentified flying objects. You decide whether they are real or not. Listen to what eye witnesses say. Are beings from other worlds visiting the Earth?"

Footage of flying saucers was shown; people from far away countries spoke of what they'd seen.

Kingsley loved the thought of strange beings travelling from one world to another in wondrous-shaped spaceships. He was so engrossed that he sat googly-eyed through the entire programme.

Spider ⚬ Seven

When the broadcast finished, Kingsley switched off the goggle-box.

It was all too much for Burrton to understand. Planets, stars and unidentified flying objects didn't fit into Burrton's world. Trying to understand about fairies was difficult enough.

Kingsley raised his arms above his head and gave an almighty yawn. "I think it's time for bed," he said.

Burrton also gave a yawn; it had been a demanding and interesting day. He was carried back to the kitchen and gently put on the windowsill.

"I'm going to practice the four rules," he said, looking at his reflection in the window.

"Pleasant dreams," said Kingsley, as he turned off the kitchen light, making the room almost as dark as the outside. As the door closed, Burrton was left looking through the window into the shadowy night.

After a wash, the brushing of teeth, and putting pyjamas on, this tired elephant was now ready for bed.

Kingsley turned off the lights and went to the bedroom window. He looked out across the countryside onto the moonlit fields. As his head tilted upwards towards silver stars, he hoped for something to happen. He saw a shooting star. What he really wanted to see was a flying saucer. *If only*, he thought, taking one last look into the heavens.

The moon was bright. Its face smiled down.

"Goodnight, Moon," said Kingsley, shutting the curtains.

As he lay in bed, with his eyelids tightly closed, he thought of other beings looking out of their bedroom windows, thinking the same.

"Goodnight," whispered the Moon.

Burrton waited patiently on the windowsill. He was looking forward to tomorrow. He wanted desperately to go home.

Burrton repeated the rules over and over again. When he could remember them, without any mistakes, he curled up like a black pea and went to sleep.

The tiny spider's dreams showed elephants being visited by beautiful fairies-helping hands revealed frightened spiders. Soft teachings calmed their fast beating hearts. Hundreds of elephants and fairies swam around in his mind; all eating huge pieces of scrumptious fruit cake. Then, flying saucers came and took the elephants and fairies away. The spiders started to cry. Their tears fell like rain; soon the windowsill was pud-dled in salty water. Then a tear collector appeared and sucked up all the tears. A tiny door opened and words walked in, they juggled themselves around to reveal the four spider rules of survival.

Things were happening in the garden. Field mice had come visiting and were nibbling at lettuces and anything they could get their teeth into–Kingsley didn't mind because there was plenty for everyone. Hedgehogs had also come and were looking for worms. The slugs had finally made their way back to the cabbages. Frogs leapt and waited, and then leapt again. Those in the garden were full of activity. Those in the house were fast asleep.

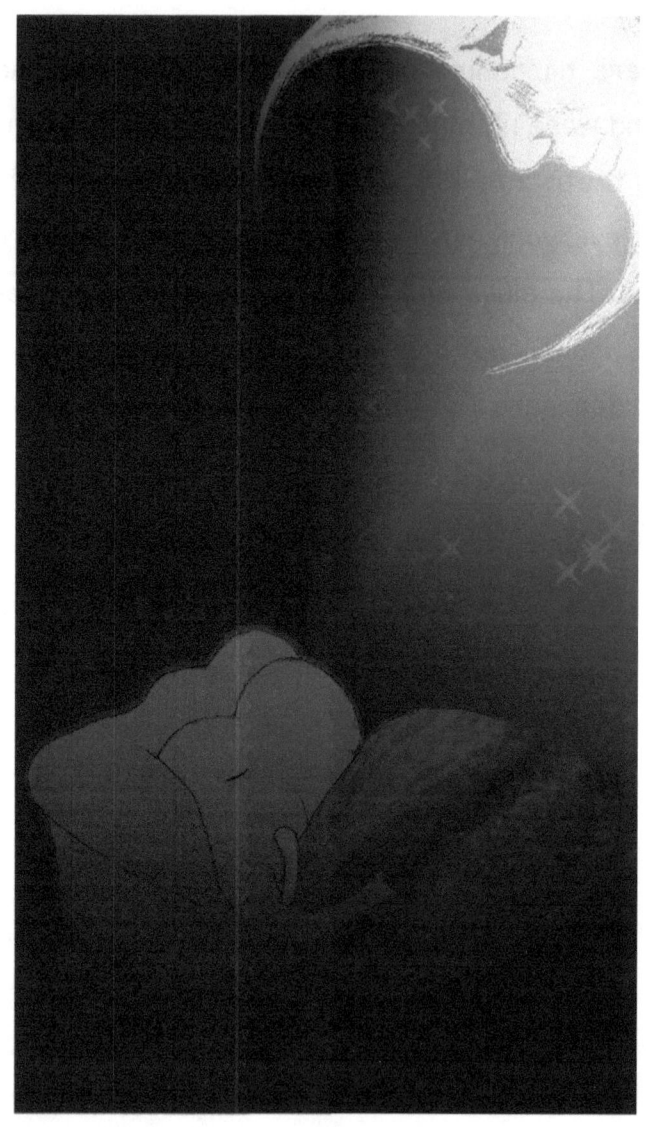

Spider Eight

Kingsley woke before the dawn. He got out of bed and put on his blue dressing gown and square-shaped slippers, and came down the stairs into the kitchen.

"Morning, Burrton," he said, as he turned on the light, making the kitchen suddenly bright.

Burrton jumped. He'd forgotten where he was. He was having another strange dream; blue people with lots of eyes were shaking all his legs, saying 'Great!'

Kingsley gave a big smile as he started to make his morning tea. "Fancy a brew?" he asked.

"No, thank you. I've drank from the plughole," Burrton answered.

"Disgusting," said Kingsley.

"It's not. I only drink from the plughole as it's always fresh from the tap," Burrton specified. "I couldn't drink anything that looks like something a cockroach has pooed in."

"I happen to like cockroach-poo tea," said Kingsley.

"Are you kidding me?" asked Burrton.

Just then the kettle whistled.

A special elephant took his mug of tea and stood by the back door; the birds were singing their good mornings, just like they always did. The lemon-coloured sun was just starting to climb the sky.

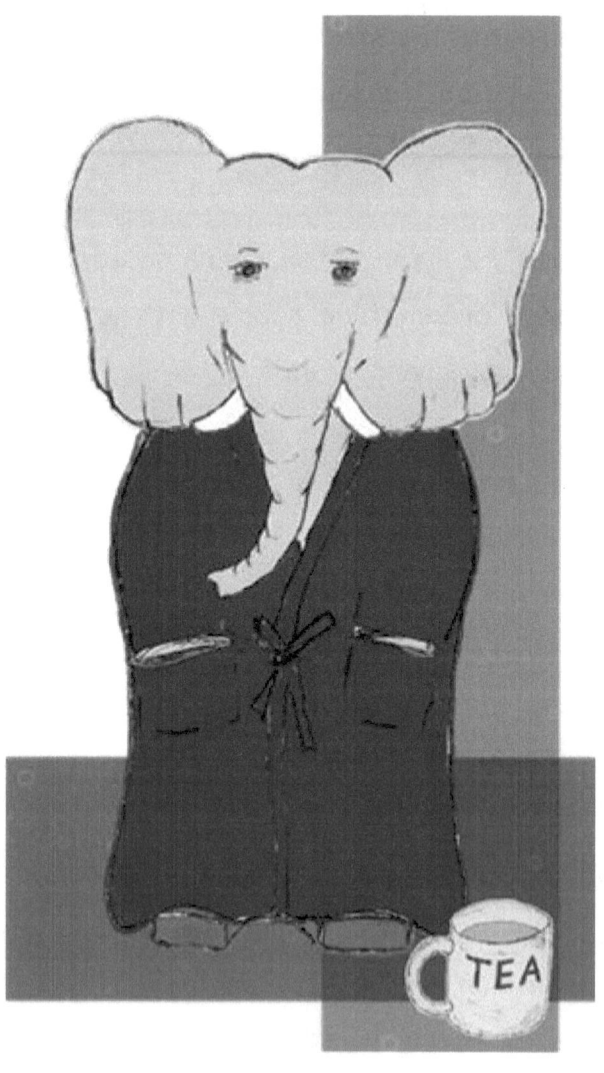

Burrton looked out of the window. "Is Miranda coming today?" he called.

"Yes, possibly," said Kingsley, coming back inside and putting his empty mug next to the yellow teapot.

"When will she come?" asked Burrton excitedly.

"Only when you're ready," said Kingsley, pouring himself another mug of tea.

"I'm ready, I'm ready," pleaded Burrton.

"Very well, Burrton, what are the four rules of spider survival?" asked Kingsley, removing the drawing from the windowsill so Burrton couldn't cheat.

"If I see anyone or hear anyone, I must always stay hidden. Rule 1: stay hidden," declared Burrton.

"Correct," said Kingsley.

"If I'm seen I should never stay still. I've got to keep moving and remember to try and get into the shadows as soon as I can. Rule 2: keep moving," declared Burrton.

"Correct again," said Kingsley.

"If I'm seen and for any reason they come near me, I'm to run straight at them. Rule 3: run at them," declared Burrton.

"Excellent," said Kingsley.

"When they jump or flinch or scream or run away, that's my chance. I must get away and hide. I'm to stay hidden, because they may come back. Rule 4: hide and stay hidden," declared Burrton.

"Jumping elephants!" said Kingsley. "You're a very clever spider to remember all four rules in such a short time."

Kingsley was so pleased that he blew his trunk like a bugle while jumping up and down.

Kingsley quizzed Burrton for the next two hours. The tiny spider never once got the rules wrong.

"Can I go home now?" asked Burrton.

"Yes, you can," said Kingsley.

"HOORAY!" shouted Burrton.

Kingsley flapped his ears.

Burrton laughed so much that he nearly toppled off the windowsill.

Spider 🕷 Nine

Burrton watched Kingsley remove a rectangular tin box, about the size of a thick-sliced loaf of bread, from the cupboard and place it on the kitchen table.

Kingsley sat down and prized open the lid. The tin box seemed to crackle and sparkle as he carefully lifted out a clear glass sphere.

"What's that?" asked Burrton.

"It's a word porter," said Kingsley honestly.

"What does it do?" asked Burrton.

Kingsley swallowed hard and sighed deeply as if he was going to try and explain the workings of a clock, but couldn't. "Well," he said. "It's like a postbox, only the letter you write is not written on paper and you don't post it... you'll understand soon enough." He looked at Burrton curiously. "Do you know you're the first to ask about it?"

"Am I?" said Burrton. "Sorry!"

"No, don't be," said Kingsley. "If you never ask, you never learn."

Burrton grinned and shuffled nervously, altogether feeling rather embarrassed.

Kingsley took from the tin a neatly folded black cloth. He laid it flat, next to the word porter. The cloth rippled like liquid ink. Then, very carefully, he picked up the word porter and placed it upon the top half of the cloth. It disappeared into blackness.

With all magic things there is transformation...

The rippling blackness began to crystalise into a thin white layer. The word porter presented itself again. It hovered and spun, and filled with an orange mist.

Burrton held his breath...

The last thing to come out of the tin box was an ordinary-looking pencil. Kingsley wrote on the thin white layer:

Dear Miranda,

Please collect a tiny spider that is ready to return home.

Kind regards, Kingsley.

Within seconds of writing, the words turned silvery blue and glistened brightly. In turn, each letter vanished and reappeared within the orange mist. The word porter set afire. The flames changed colour from red to blue to yellow to green, filling the kitchen in multi-coloured light.

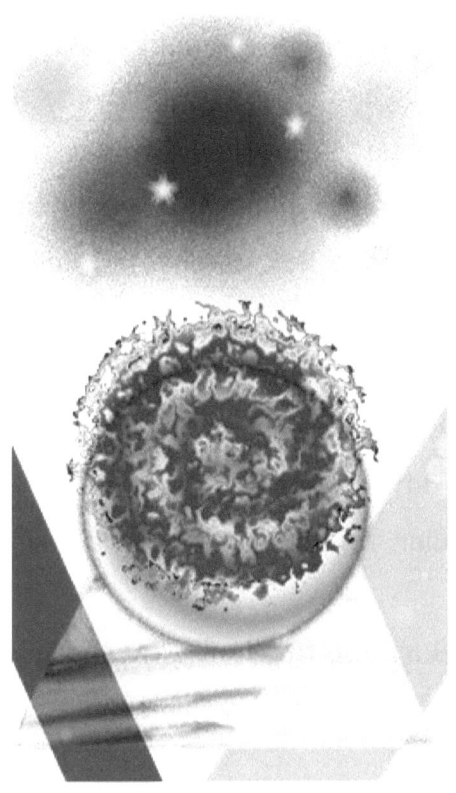

The statically-charged air crackled with zing, and then exploded with a pop. It was so loud that Kingsley's ears numbed for several seconds.

"I'm still getting used to that bit," he said, flapping his ears.

The tiny hairs on Burrton's legs sizzled like rashers of bacon being fried. He tried shaking his legs, but it didn't help.

The word porter returned to clear. It hovered without spinning.

Kingsley took hold of the clear glass sphere and carefully placed it back in the tin box.

Burrton watched as the thin white layer return to liquid ink.

Kingsley picked up the cloth and folded it away beside the sphere. The last thing to go back in the tin box was the ordinary-looking pencil. The lid was pressed down to keep in the magic.

"It won't be long now," he said. "Miranda will be on her way as soon as she reads the letter."

Burrton said nothing. He was speechless.

The rectangular tin box was returned safely to the cupboard.

"Wow!" said Burrton, finally finding his voice.

"Wow, indeed!" said Kingsley. "They all say that."

Spider 🕷 Ten

Kingsley went upstairs to get dressed for the day.

Burrton nervously looked out of the window and waited for Miranda to arrive. He didn't have to wait long. From somewhere between the runner beans and the lettuce patch a flash of silver and blue sparked the air.

Burrton's eyes shone with excitement. "MIRANDA'S HERE!" he yelled.

Kingsley rushed into the kitchen wearing his favourite gardening clothes of a tee-shirt and dungarees. "Blimey! If that isn't the quickest yet," he said, opening the back door.

"Hello, Kingsley," called Miranda, skipping down the garden towards him. She glowed radiantly. Her dark beauty, shimmering magically, was letting the lemon-coloured sun shine through her as if its rays were forbidden to touch.

"Good morning, Miranda," said Kingsley, bowing very politely. "It's always such a pleasure to see you."

"You, too," said Miranda, smiling up at her special elephant. "He must be a fast learner."

"He is," said Kingsley, leading Miranda into the kitchen.

Miranda sat on her usual chair–the one piled high with gardening books. "Hello, tiny spider," she said, smiling across at Burrton.

"Hello," said Burrton shyly.

"Would you like a drink, Miranda?" asked Kingsley.

"Some gooseberry juice would be nice," she said.

"Of course," said Kingsley. He went to the cupboard and brought out a bottle of his prized gooseberry juice. A goblet-the one that was especially made for fairies-was filled to the brim and handed over with loving pride.

Kingsley also took from the cupboard a large jam roll. He cut himself and Miranda a slice each. The crumbly bits he gave to Burrton.

Miranda delicately ate her slice of jam roll and drank her gooseberry juice. "So this tiny spider wants to go home, does he?" she asked.

Kingsley's mouth was so full of cake that he could only nod.

"Oh, yes, please," said Burrton, getting so excited that he nearly toppled off the windowsill for a second time.

Miranda laughed and walked over to Burrton. She held out her hand and Burrton scurried on.

"Then it's time to say goodbye," said Miranda, cradling the tiny spider.

"Bye, Kingsley, and thank you," Burrton said.

"Bye-bye, Burrton," said Kingsley. "Don't forget everything I've taught you."

Miranda closed her hand carefully around the tiny spider and walked out into the garden. "Time to go," she said.

"Goodbye, Miranda," said Kingsley.

"Bye for now, Kingsley, see you again, soon," said Miranda.

High into the air she soared, where she quickly vanished from view.

Kingsley emptied the yellow teapot into the bucket under the sink. Teapot and mug were washed and put away.

Now, he thought, *that front garden. I better get started on it; it's no use putting it off any longer.*

It was a hot day; the morning's lemon-coloured sun was now a ball of afternoon orange–it shone down on Kingsley as he worked hard deadheading the roses and pulling up those forever growing weeds. He was still undecided as what to do best.

Shall I leave it as a rose garden or make it a vegetable garden? he questioned. He knew he needed the room if he was to grow more cabbages.

That night, the house of red bricks, with its vegetable garden to the back and rose garden to the front, felt lonely without a spider to teach.

"Goodnight, Moon," said Kingsley, shutting the curtains.

As he lay in bed, with his eyelids tightly closed, he thought about Burrton and hoped the tiny spider could still remember the rules of survival.

Burrton crept across the floor of a dark room.

A door opened. Incoming light slashed across the floor. It struck like lightening.

Burrton's teensy-weensy heart beat like a drum.

A piercing scream, followed by running away feet, and the shrieking of, "There's a spider," filled the night silence.

Rule 2: keep moving, thought Burrton.

Into the room ran vile Victor, followed by his sister.

Shrieking Shirley pointed at Burrton. "It's there," she said, squirming. "Isn't it horrid, hairy and big?"

I'm not horrid, thought Burrton, as he scurried for the shadows. *And I'm not big, and I'm only a little hairy.*

A dark shadow towered over the tiny spider. Victor had his rolled-up comic again.

Burrton couldn't move fast enough. *Rule 3: run at them,* he thought. And then, with every ounce of energy he had, he ran at the boy.

Victor saw the spider rush towards him. He gave a piercing scream and jumped a mile.

"Jumping elephants!" cried Burrton. "It worked!"

Burrton took this moment and ran and ran. He hid behind a chair leg and then under the skirting board.

It was there, in the dark that he thought.

But what, you might ask, was this tiny spider thinking?

It was this:

The spider rules do work. He was right about them jumping a mile. He is indeed a very special elephant. Thank you, Kingsley.

Late one night, a shoe hit the floor with such a THUD that it made a tiny spider stop stone-dead. The tiny spider's teensy-weensy heart almost stopped.

The shoe was lifted into the air again–this time, ready to land right on top of the tiny spider.

Without warning, a flash of light appeared and the spider was whisked away within twinkling silver and blue lights.

"You're safe now, tiny spider," said a voice that seemed to come from nowhere. "Don't be afraid. Everything will be al-right."

Kingsley would soon be teaching another tiny spider the rules of survival.

If you're lucky enough to hear a spider talk, then you'll know it was once saved by Miranda the Spider Fairy. And, therefore, it must have remembered the rules taught by her very special elephant, Kingsley Trunk.

Poor Kingsley looks sad; he knows that lots of small creatures die because of someone being horrid to them.

Everyone should think before raising a comic, newspaper, book or shoe in their attempt to squash another living creature.

After all, everything has a right to life; even a tiny spider!

Kingsley Trunk

How did Gruvel come to be on the Gregorys' doorstep?

Where has Gruvel come from?

And what on earth are they going to do with Gruvel?

As the family try to answer these questions,
Gruvel teaches them a wonderful lesson.

For more information
visit: www.speakingvolumes.us

The story unfolds alongside a catchy rhyme
and delightful illustrations as Patrick
goes on a journey of discovery.

For more information
visit: www.speakingvolumes.us

I'd like to go back in time, to put hurtful wrongs to right.
My advice: make time for the ones you love

A donkey, a letter, and a bottle of clear liquid
all combine to make 'The Secret'.

For more information
visit: www.speakingvolumes.us

**One evening, my whisperer said the name 'Arthur Runkin'.
My imagination was alight!**

**Imagine knowing something about yourself.
And all because of a suitcase.**

Written and Illustrated by
L. Sydney Abel

Published by SpeakingVolumes

For more information
visit: www.speakingvolumes.us

Can wolves change colour?

Do pixies exist?

According to Mr. Hedges they do.

Written and Illustrated by
L. Sydney Abel

For more information
visit: www.speakingvolumes.us

**Daydreaming about pirate adventures transports
'Then' to 'Now'**

**Sleepin' be one thing an' dreamin' be another.
But when dreamin' walks into yer wakin'
then that be something altogether diff'rent.**

For more information
visit: www.speakingvolumes.us

Under Nelida Wellington's stairs lives a Jinny-Yen.
Only children can see such creatures.
A Jinny-Yen is a Wish Granter.

And for most boys and girls, their thoughts turn to greed.
But not all children are devoured by greed...

Written and Illustrated by
L. Sydney Abel

For more information
visit: www.speakingvolumes.us

Lucretia Crumb, a girl of unusual nature, knows a thing or two and believes Ish-ish is a witch.

Ish-ish loves finger and fingernail stew.

Lucretia wants to keep all her fingers…

For more information
visit: www.speakingvolumes.us

www.ingramcontent.com/pod-product-compliance
Lightning Source LLC
Chambersburg PA
CBHW030542180626
46810CB00005B/1971